Cherry
the Cake
Fairy

For Saoirse Medway

Special thanks to

Sue Mongredien

ISBN 978-0-545-22168-9

Text copyright © 2005 by Rainbow Magic Limited.
Illustrations copyright © 2005 by Georgie Ripper.

12 11 10 9 8 7 6 5 4 3 2 1   10 11 12 13 14 15/0

Printed in the U.S.A.   40

First Scholastic Printing, July 2010

Cherry
the Cake
Fairy

by Daisy Meadows

SCHOLASTIC INC.

New York   Toronto   London   Auckland

Sydney   Mexico City   New Delhi   Hong Kong

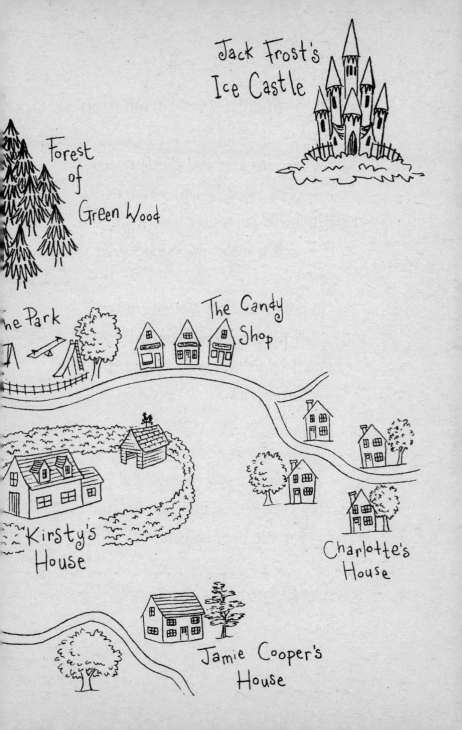

A Very Special Party Invitation

Our gracious king and gentle queen
Are loved by fairies all.
One thousand years they have ruled well,
Through troubles great and small.

In honor of their glorious reign
A party has been planned.
We'll celebrate their anniversary
Throughout all of Fairyland.

The party is a royal surprise,
We hope they'll be delighted.
So pull out your wand and fanciest dress . . .
For *you* have been invited!

RSVP: THE FAIRY GODMOTHER

Contents

A Birthday Surprise

"I just know this is going to be a wonderful birthday!" Kirsty Tate exclaimed happily, her eyes shining.

Mrs. Tate laughed across the breakfast table. "You've only been awake for half an hour, Kirsty," she said.

"I know," Kirsty replied. "But look at all these cards I've gotten already! Plus, there's my party this afternoon. And best of all, Rachel's here for a whole week!" She grinned at her best friend, Rachel

Walker, who was sitting next to her. The two girls were spending spring break together. They had met on a vacation to Rainspell Island and, since then, they had shared all kinds of magical adventures. First, they had helped all seven of the Rainbow Fairies return to Fairyland. Then, they'd helped the Weather Fairies stop wicked Jack Frost from causing weather chaos—and that was just the beginning of their fairy fun!

The girls finished their breakfast
and went to get dressed. Rachel was
halfway up the stairs behind Kirsty,
when she noticed another envelope
coming through the mail slot. She ran
to get it. It was a beautiful, sparkly gold
envelope, and it felt heavy in her hand.
She glanced curiously at the front — and
then gasped in surprise. *Miss Kirsty Tate
and Miss Rachel Walker*, read the beautiful
loopy handwriting. Rachel blinked.
A card for Kirsty
and for her? But
it wouldn't be
her birthday for
another three
months!

Rachel raced

up the stairs two at a time, thinking about the card. She didn't recognize the handwriting, so it couldn't be from her mom or dad. But who else knew that she was staying with Kirsty?

"Look," cried Rachel, bursting into Kirsty's bedroom. "Another card—and it's for both of us!"

Kirsty took the envelope and gently turned it over, running her finger around the red wax seal on the back. "You open it," she said, passing the letter back to Rachel and smiling. "I've gotten lots of cards this morning."

Rachel's fingers trembled with excitement as she carefully broke the wax seal. As soon as the envelope was open, glittering clouds of fairy dust floated into the air, followed by

a rainbow that soared across the room.

Both girls stared, their mouths wide open. Riding on top of the rainbow, as if he were surfing on a wave, was Bertram, the frog footman from Fairyland! Rachel and Kirsty had met him on their earlier fairy adventures. But they hadn't expected to see him again in Kirsty's bedroom!

Bertram hopped off the rainbow onto Kirsty's dresser and took a grand bow. He wore a red vest and carried a gold bugle.

Kirsty grabbed Rachel's hand and squeezed it. She couldn't help wondering if this would be the start of another magical quest!

Bertram tooted on the bugle, then
pulled a tiny scroll from one of his
pockets. He unrolled it, and cleared his
throat. "*Ahem.* It is with great pleasure,"
he began, "that I
bring you good
news. The Fairy
Godmother hereby
invites Kirsty
Tate and Rachel
Walker to a surprise
party—for the fairy
king and queen's 1000th anniversary as
wise rulers of Fairyland!"

"Wow!" Rachel gasped.

"Hooray!" Kirsty cried.

From another one of his pockets,
Bertram pulled out a tiny bag of fairy
dust and began sprinkling it over Kirsty's

mirror. As the girls watched, the mirror's reflection vanished and a whole new scene appeared before their eyes.

"It's Fairyland!" Rachel breathed, leaning closer for a better look.

"Correct," said Bertram. "The Fairy Party Workshop, to be precise. All the Party Fairies have been working very hard to make sure the king and queen's party is absolutely perfect."

Kirsty and Rachel gazed in delight at the small figures they could see rushing around the workshop.

"There's Cherry the Cake Fairy, making a special party cake," Bertram told them, pointing a webbed green finger. The cake looked wonderful. It was shaped like a fairy palace and it sparkled with magic. "That's Grace the Glitter Fairy, making lots of magical decorations. And can you see the fairy wrapping up the pretty gifts? That's Jasmine the Present Fairy."

The two girls watched in delight as Jasmine tied a pink satin ribbon around one of the presents.

"Who else is there?" Kirsty asked eagerly.

Bertram pointed. "There's Polly the Party Fun Fairy. She's in charge of party games. And Melodie the Music Fairy selects the best party tunes. She's teaching the fairy orchestra how to play the harmonies for 'Happy Anniversary.'" The girls fell silent and listened to the sweet sounds of fairy music drifting through the mirror. "It's gorgeous!" Rachel said, sighing happily. Bertram went on, "Honey the Candy Fairy is making sure there are enough snacks for everyone, and Phoebe the Fashion Fairy—look, she's the one with the extra-sparkly wings—

is in charge of everyone's party outfits."

Kirsty gazed in wonder at the beautiful
dress Phoebe was working on. It was
covered with hundreds of sequins and
jewels that glittered in the light. "It's
gorgeous," Kirsty breathed, her eyes
wide with excitement. "And we're really
invited to the party?"

"Oh, yes," Bertram replied. "The Fairy
Godmother says that you and Rachel
will be special guests."

"Special guests!" Rachel echoed,

looking thrilled at the thought.

"So, when is the party? And how will we get there?" Kirsty asked.

Bertram murmured something at the mirror and the Fairyland scene dissolved into hundreds of twinkling stars, before finally disappearing.

"The party's at the end of the week. And the Fairy Godmother will send a magic rainbow to take you there," he said. He handed the magic invitation to Rachel. "To get to Fairyland, all you have to do is step onto the end of the rainbow," he explained, "like this."

Kirsty and Rachel watched as
Bertram placed one froggy foot,
then another, into the colorful
rainbow that floated in the air. And
then—*whoosh!*—with a shower of
golden fairy dust, he was gone.

"Hooray!" exclaimed Kirsty. "I knew this was going to be an amazing birthday."

"It looks like it's going to be *magical*," Rachel replied, grinning.

Fun and Games

Rachel and Kirsty got dressed, chatting with excitement.

"The Fairy Godmother called us 'special guests'," Rachel said proudly, pulling her hair into a ponytail. "Imagine! You and me, special guests of King Oberon and Queen Titania at their important celebration!"

"It's amazing!" Kirsty grinned, brushing her hair. "I can't wait to go to Fairyland again."

Just then, there was a shout from downstairs. "Come on, girls!" Mrs. Tate called. "There's a lot to do before the party starts."

Rachel and Kirsty looked at each other in amazement. How did Mrs. Tate know about the Fairyland party? Then Kirsty giggled. "She means *my* party," she said. "In all the fairy excitement, I almost forgot all about it for a minute!"

The girls laughed and hurried downstairs. In the kitchen, Mr. Tate was icing Kirsty's birthday cake. "There," he said, putting nine candles on top. "It's all finished."

"That looks delicious, Dad," Kirsty said, hugging him. "Come on, Rachel—let's see what Mom wants us to do."

Mrs. Tate soon had the two girls filling party bags for all of Kirsty's guests. Then they blew up lots of pink and lilac balloons to hang from the ceiling. And finally, there was just enough time for the girls to put on their party dresses before the guests started to arrive.

"Let's play Musical Statues first," Mrs.

Tate announced to all the girls gathered in the family room. "When the music stops—so do you!" The music started and everybody danced. Then Mr. Tate turned it off—and everybody froze on the spot. Rachel was standing on one leg, trying to keep as still as possible, when she suddenly saw swirls of red and purple glitter floating through the doorway. She stared in surprise, wondering what it could be.

Then she glanced to the side, wondering if Kirsty had spotted the glitter, too. Kirsty looked startled, so Rachel was sure that she had. Luckily, none of the other girls seemed to have noticed anything unusual.

The sparkling dust floated over to Rachel, drifting right under her nose. "Achoo! Achoo! Achoo!" she sneezed.

Now the dust was near Kirsty, too. It was so ticklish! She just couldn't help rubbing her nose.

"Rachel and Kirsty—you two are out!" Mrs. Tate said. "Here comes the music again."

As quickly as they had appeared, the
swirls of red and purple glitter vanished.
Rachel frowned at Kirsty. "What was
that?" she whispered as they went to sit
down.

Kirsty grabbed her arm and steered
her toward the door. "I think it might
have had something to do with her,"
she whispered, pointing through the
doorway.

Rachel followed Kirsty's finger, and a broad smile spread over her face. It was just like she had hoped. There, hovering in midair and waving at the girls, was a tiny sparkling fairy!

Stop, Thief!

"You're one of the Party Fairies!" Rachel
exclaimed as they rushed over to the little
fairy. "We saw you in Bertram's picture."

The fairy smiled. She had sparkly, deep
violet eyes and long, dark, curly hair that
was tied in pigtails with red ribbons. She
wore a red skirt, a pink wrap top, red
party shoes, and striped socks. A sparkly

red party bag dangled from her wrist. "I
certainly am," she replied, with a curtsy.
"I'm Cherry the Cake Fairy!" An anxious
frown creased her
forehead. "I'm
sorry if my fairy
dust ruined your
game," she went
on, "but I really
need your help!"

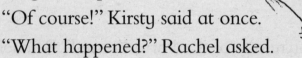

"Of course!" Kirsty said at once.

"What happened?" Rachel asked.

Cherry smiled gratefully. "Well, you
see, as the Cake Fairy, whenever there is
danger that a cake might be ruined, I get
called away from Fairyland to fix it. And
I've been very busy today. One of Jack
Frost's goblins has been ruining birthday
cakes all over the place! He steals the cake

candles, and stomps in the icing." She bit her lip. "And he's on his way to your party right now, Kirsty!"

Rachel's mouth fell open. "What a mess!" she exclaimed.

Kirsty glanced over at the kitchen door. "Why is the goblin ruining all the cakes?" she asked. "And what can we do to stop him?"

Cherry's eyes flashed. "Nobody knows what the goblin is up to," she told the girls. "But one thing's for sure—if Jack Frost is behind it, it must be something bad." She shrugged. "We have to catch the goblin before he causes any more trouble."

"What are we waiting for?" Rachel cried. "Let's guard Kirsty's cake right now!"

The girls raced to the kitchen, with Cherry fluttering behind them. But as soon as they opened the kitchen door, it was clear that they were too late. All the candles had been pulled out of Kirsty's cake, and there were goblin footprints in the icing.

"Oh, no!" cried Kirsty in dismay. "He ruined it!"

"He took all the candles," Rachel added angrily.

"And I'll take this, too!" somebody cackled. Before anyone could stop him, a grinning green goblin jumped out from behind one of the table legs, snatched Cherry's party bag out of her hands, and ran off.

A Tricky Problem

"Hey!" Cherry cried. "Give that back!"

Kirsty and Rachel stared in horror as the goblin ran away. He was his normal Fairyland size, Rachel realized with relief. At least Jack Frost hadn't cast a spell to make the goblins bigger, like he'd done before. An enormous backpack bumped up and down, weighing on the goblin's

shoulders. The bag was stuffed so full of
birthday candles that the top couldn't
even close!

"We have to get my party bag back!"
Cherry cried, flying after the thief.
"Quick!"

The goblin was just about to dodge
through the kitchen door, when Kirsty's

kitten, Pearl, came bounding into the
room. As soon as Pearl
saw the goblin, her
black-and-white fur
stood up in alarm,
and the kitten hissed.

The goblin's
eyes opened wide
in panic, and he
skidded to a halt.
Then he climbed into one of the kitchen
cupboards and locked himself in!

Cherry flitted in the air anxiously.
"That party bag has all my magical
fairy dust inside," she said, worried.
"I need it to help make parties
perfect—and to finish the king and
queen's anniversary cake."

Rachel banged on the cupboard door.

"Give that party bag back to Cherry right now!" she ordered the goblin.

"No way," the goblin shouted back grumpily. "It's mine now! As soon as I get out of here, I'm giving it to Jack Frost."

"Why does he want it?" Kirsty asked. The goblin gave a nasty laugh. "For his party, of course," he replied. "The king and queen said he has to stay in his ice castle, but they didn't say he couldn't have a party of his own. It will be a very fancy one, too! Now that I have this party bag of magic dust, his cake is going to be the most magnificent cake you've ever seen." There was another cackle from the cupboard. "Just you wait—once we have all the Party Fairies' party bags, Jack Frost will use the magic dust to make his party extra-special."

Cherry turned very pale. She motioned for the girls to come back over to the table, where they huddled together.

"It's bad enough that he has my party bag when I haven't finished the king and queen's cake," she said. "But if the goblins are planning to steal *all* of the magic party bags, then none of the Party Fairies will be able to finish their work in time for the anniversary party!"

Cherry's wings drooped, and she shook her head in misery. "The surprise party will be ruined!"

Rachel and Kirsty looked at their sad fairy friend. What could they do to help?

A Sticky Solution

The girls tried hard to figure out a way to get Cherry's party bag back. But they couldn't think of anything!

"The Fairy Godmother is much more powerful than a goblin," Cherry said, sighing. "She'd be able to fix this problem if I could just get the goblin back to Fairyland. But I can't use my

magic to send him back while he's
hiding in that cupboard—or while he's
running away. I need to be able to see
him, and he has to stay very still, so that
I can wave my wand over him."

Kirsty found her gaze drifting toward
her ruined birthday cake. "Poor Dad. He
spent ages on that icing,"
she said sadly.
Suddenly, she grinned
as a thought came
to her. "That's it!" she
muttered. "That's how
we'll get him out!"
"How?" Rachel
asked, confused.

"We need to make more icing for
this cake," Kirsty said loudly, so the
goblin would hear. She took out a box

of powdered sugar and started mixing
some icing in a bowl. Then she added
quietly, "Cherry, could you use your
fairy magic to make this icing
extra-sticky?"

"No problem,"
Cherry replied. She
waved her wand
over the bowl,
and a stream of
sparkling purple
and red fairy dust

swirled around it. The white icing
glittered for a split-second, and strange
red and purple sparks crackled above
it. Then the icing turned glossy white
again.

Kirsty gave one last stir and smiled.
"Super-sticky!" she whispered.

Rachel was still frowning. "I don't—" she began.

But Kirsty put a finger to her lips. "It's a trap!" she whispered into Rachel's ear. Quickly, she covered the cake with the new icing. "We'd better get back to the party now that the cake is frosted again. We'll just leave it here on the table . . ." she said loudly.

Rachel and Cherry
followed Kirsty
out of the room.
Holding their breath,
they waited outside
the kitchen, peeking
through the crack in
the door to see if Kirsty's
trap would work. Rachel crossed her fingers.

Sure enough, after a moment, the
cupboard door creaked open.
The goblin climbed
down and skipped
happily across the floor.
With a nasty grin,
he climbed up onto
the kitchen table, and
took a giant leap straight onto
the top of the newly-iced cake.

"There he goes," Kirsty whispered to Rachel. "And any second now, he'll realize . . ."

"I'm stuck!" the goblin howled suddenly. "They tricked me!"

"Perfect timing!" Cherry giggled.

The goblin couldn't move his feet in the super-sticky icing. Rachel laughed out loud at the furious look on his face. "Great idea, Kirsty," she cheered.

Cherry flew over to the goblin,
her eyes glued to her precious
party bag. As soon as he
saw her, he bared
his teeth. "If you
get any closer,
fairy, I'll bite
you!" he warned.

"In that case,
I'll have to take
you back to
Fairyland," Cherry
said calmly. "I think the Fairy
Godmother will be interested to find
out what you and Jack Frost have been
plotting."

The goblin scowled, but said no more.

"Serves you right for ruining my
cake—twice!" Kirsty added.

"Don't worry about your cake, Kirsty," Cherry said. "Once I have my party bag back, I'll use my magic to make you the most beautiful birthday cake you've ever seen. Now, would you two would like to come to Fairyland with me?"

"Yes, please!" Kirsty cried at once, but Rachel was glancing up at the kitchen clock.

"What about your party, Kirsty?" she pointed out. "The Musical Statues game has to be over soon."

Cherry twirled her wand around. "Don't worry," she said, "I'll work some magic. It will seem like you've only been gone from the party for a moment! Will that help?"

"Oh, yes!" cried both girls together.

"I was hoping you'd say that." Cherry smiled. "Off we go!"

A Magical Mystery Cake!

With a blur of bright colors — and
the delicious smell of freshly-baked
cakes — Kirsty and Rachel found
themselves flying through the air
toward Fairyland.

"Hello," a sweet voice called as they
landed with a bump. "Which one of you
is Kirsty and which one is Rachel? I've

heard so much about you, my dears."

Kirsty and Rachel blinked and looked
around. They were in Fairyland, and
both girls were now fairy-size themselves.
They even had wings! And there,
standing in front of them, was somebody
who could only be the Fairy Godmother.
She had long, copper-colored hair held
back by her crown, the kindest green
eyes that Rachel and Kirsty had ever
seen, and wings that shimmered every

time they moved. Her long golden dress was covered in tiny glimmering jewels that twinkled in all the colors of the rainbow.

"I'm Kirsty," Kirsty said, jumping up at once.

"And I'm Rachel," Rachel added, scrambling to her feet.

"Delighted to meet you at last," the Fairy Godmother replied, bending into a beautiful curtsy.

Her eyes narrowed at the sight of the goblin, who was standing next to Cherry. "I see you've taken something that doesn't belong to you," she said sternly, pointing a finger at Cherry's party bag.

The party bag glowed with red and purple light, then shot out of the goblin's hands. It zoomed straight over to Cherry, who grabbed it with relief.

"Thank you!" she cried.

"You're welcome, my dear," the Fairy Godmother said. Then she fixed her gaze

on the goblin. "As for you,
I know the perfect way
to teach you a lesson."
She pointed a finger
at the goblin. "You'll
need that," she said,
"and that."
Kirsty and Rachel
couldn't help laughing
as an enormous chef's hat
appeared on the goblin's head, and a
crisp white apron wrapped
itself around his body.

"You can help in the
Party Workshop for the
rest of the week, icing all
the cakes," the Fairy
Godmother insisted. "Let's

hope that keeps you out of trouble."

The goblin pouted as Cherry led him
away. "You won't catch the other goblins
as easily," he snarled. "They'll get the rest
of the party bags, just you wait and see!"

Once he had gone, the Fairy

Godmother turned back to Kirsty and Rachel. "I'm afraid he might be right," she told them. "Jack Frost's goblins can be very clever, as you know. They'll try every trick they know to steal the other magic party bags."

"What can we do to help?" Kirsty asked.

The Fairy Godmother smiled. "All you can do is look out for trouble at parties," she said. "The goblins will probably try to cause problems at human parties, because they know that the Party Fairies will rush to help. That will give them a chance to steal the fairies' party bags."

"We'll keep a lookout," Rachel
promised.

Just then, Cherry returned. "We'd better
send you back to your party," she told
the girls. "And don't worry—I'm sure
there won't be any more goblins spoiling
your fun today." She carefully opened
her party bag and reached inside. The
Fairy Godmother pointed her wand
at the girls and called, "Home!" At the
same time, Cherry threw a handful of
red and purple
fairy dust over
them.

The world
seemed to spin,
there was a
sweet, sugary
smell in the air,

and then the girls found themselves back
in Kirsty's kitchen.

"Jessica's the winner!" they heard Mrs.
Tate saying. "Come and get your prize
for being the best statue, Jessica."

"It sounds like the game just finished,"
Kirsty said happily, "just like Cherry
promised. Let's go and join the party
again, Rachel."

But Rachel was staring at the kitchen table with wonder. "Kirsty!" she cried. "Look at your cake!"

Kirsty gasped in surprise. The red and purple fairy dust that Cherry had thrown over them was floating down onto the cake that Mr. Tate had made—and the goblin had trampled. As the fairy dust landed on the cake, something amazing happened. A delicious fragrance of vanilla and sugar floated around the room, and the original cake melted into thin air. Instantly, a new cake formed in its place. Kirsty and

Rachel stared in wonder as three layers appeared, one by one, beautifully covered with white, pink, and purple icing. Each layer was decorated with tiny sugar fairies, vines of sugar roses, and shiny silver bells. Kirsty broke the silence with a sudden laugh. "It's the Party Fairies!" she cried, pointing at the sugar figures. "See? There's Cherry with a wooden spoon, and the Glitter Fairy, didn't Bertram say her name was Grace? And a fairy with a present—that must be Jasmine. And—"

Suddenly, they heard Mrs. Tate calling

for them. "Kirsty! Rachel! Where are you?"

"Time to go," Rachel said. "Should we take the cake in with us, just to be on the safe side?"

"Good idea," said Kirsty. Then she grinned. "I can't wait to see everybody's faces!"

Very carefully, the girls lifted the magnificent cake. As they carried it into the living room together, the little silver bells tinkled happily.

"Wow!" cried Kirsty's friend Jessica. "I've never seen anything like it."

Another girl, Molly, was licking her lips. "It's almost too beautiful to eat," she said. "But it smells so delicious, I'll just have to give it a try!"

Mrs. Tate looked dazzled. "It's a work of art!" she said to her husband in amazement.

Mr. Tate was staring at the cake with a bewildered expression on his face. "Well . . . um . . . It's not too hard to make, when you know how," he said sheepishly.

"I can't wait to see what you're going to do for my birthday next month!" Mrs. Tate added. Mr. Tate looked alarmed at that, so Kirsty quickly interrupted. "Can we cut the cake now, Mom?"

"Good idea," Mrs. Tate replied. She lit the candles, and everybody sang "Happy Birthday." Then Kirsty carefully sliced into the lowest layer of the cake. As she did, hundreds of magical butterflies

fluttered into the room. Their colorful
wings sparkled in the sunshine.

"*Ooooh!*" everybody exclaimed, as the
butterflies vanished into thin air. "Just
like magic!"

Kirsty and Rachel smiled at each other. They both knew that it *was* magic—fairy magic, the most wonderful kind in the world!

As they took bites of the delicious birthday cake, they both couldn't help thinking about their new fairy mission.

"I can't wait to meet the other Party Fairies," Rachel whispered to Kirsty. "But I'm not looking forward to seeing any more goblins."

"I know," Kirsty agreed. "I just hope we can keep them from ruining the king and queen's party."

Rachel patted her friend's arm. "At least Cherry said there'd be no more trouble at your party," she pointed out. "So we can enjoy the rest of your birthday without worrying."

Kirsty nodded. "Yes," she said and grinned. "An invitation to the king and queen's anniversary party, meeting Cherry, and a visit to Fairyland—I knew this was going to be a wonderful birthday," she sighed happily. "And I was right!"

THE PARTY FAIRIES

Cherry has her magic
party bag back. Now Rachel
and Kirsty must help

Melodie

the Music Fairy!

Join their next adventure
in this special sneak peek . . .

Musical Mayhem

"Kirsty, you're an amazing dancer!"
Rachel Walker smiled, clapping her hands
as her friend took a bow. Kirsty had just
finished practicing the ballet steps she
would be performing later that evening.

"It will look even better tonight, when
I'm with the other dancers and everyone
is in costume," Kirsty replied with a grin.

"And wait till you hear the beautiful music."

Rachel was staying with her best friend, Kirsty Tate, for the week. That evening, the girls were going to the village hall for a very special occasion — the first anniversary of Kirsty's ballet school.

"It's going to be a great party," Kirsty went on. "My ballet teacher decorated the hall and is organizing some games, and all the parents are bringing food."

"It sounds like fun," Rachel agreed. "But if it's a party, then we'll have to be on the lookout for goblins!"

Suddenly, the girls heard Mrs. Tate's voice. "Time to go, girls!" she called.

Kirsty and Rachel hurried downstairs

to join Kirsty's mom and dad.

Mr. Tate held up a cake tin. "I made cupcakes for the party," he explained, lifting the lid.

"Cupcakes, my favorite!" Rachel said with delight. "You couldn't have made anything better."

"Thanks, Dad," Kirsty grinned, carefully taking the tin.

Mr. Tate drove them all to the village hall. They arrived to find it already full of friends and families who had come to join the celebration.

"The hall looks so different!" Kirsty gasped. Several rows of chairs had been set up to face the stage, just like in a real theater. Shiny silver streamers hung from the ceiling, twinkling Christmas lights bordered the stage, and bunches of silver and white balloons floated above each table of food.

While Mr. and Mrs. Tate chatted with other parents, Rachel and Kirsty arranged the cupcakes on a plate. They weren't the only things that looked delicious.

"Yum, chocolate éclairs!" Kirsty pointed out. Then she frowned. "They look almost too good to be true."

"Maybe we should test some of these—just to make sure the food hasn't been spoiled by a goblin!" Rachel suggested.

RAINBOW magic ™

There's Magic in Every Series!

The Rainbow Fairies

The Weather Fairies

The Jewel Fairies

The Pet Fairies

The Fun Day Fairies

The Petal Fairies

The Dance Fairies

The Music Fairies

The Sports Fairies

The Party Fairies

Read them all!

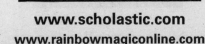

www.scholastic.com

www.rainbowmagiconline.com

HIT entertainment

RMFAIRY2